Max is **very** sleepy.

Max has drunk his milk.

Max has brushed his teeth.

Max has cleaned behind his ears.

Now Max is going to say goodnight . . .

'Goodnight Fish,'
says Max.

'Goodnight Box,'
says Max.

'Goodnight Spider,' says Max.

'Goodnight Moon,'
says Max.

But the moon is
nowhere to be seen.

'Moon . . .
Moon!
Where are you Moon?'
says Max.

'Maybe I'll see Moon from outside . . .'

Max steps out into the starlit night.

'Goodnight Night,' says Max.
'Have you seen Moon?'

But the night is dark and quiet.

'Maybe I'll see Moon if I get

a little higher,' thinks Max.

Max tiptoes carefully up onto the sleeping dog.

'Goodnight Dog,' whispers Max.
'Have you seen Moon?'

But the sleeping dog is sleeping.

'Maybe I'll see Moon if I get
a little higher,' thinks Max.

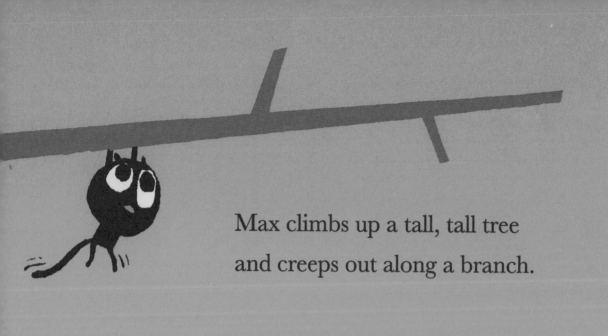

Max climbs up a tall, tall tree
and creeps out along a branch.

'Goodnight Tree,' says Max. 'Do you
know where I can find Moon?'

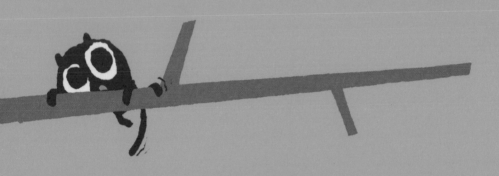

But the tall, tall tree only rustles in the breeze.

Max climbs even higher, up amongst the rooftops.

'Goodnight Rooftops,' says Max.
'Have **you** seen Moon?'

But the rooftops are silent.

'Hmm, maybe if I get much higher . . .'
thinks Max. 'Maybe from the tallest building?'

Max climbs up

and up

and up.

'Goodnight Tallest Building,' says Max.

'Can you see Moon?'

But the tallest building says nothing.

'Oh, Moon.
Where **are** you Moon?'
says Max.

Max is very tired, but he climbs up
even higher,
　　to the **highest** of the high hills,
　　　　where the wind blows cold and strong.

'Goodnight Hill,' says Max.
'Please tell me, have you seen Moon?'

But the highest of the high hills
just whistles in the wind.

Max has had enough . . .

Moooooooooon!

Where are yoooouu?

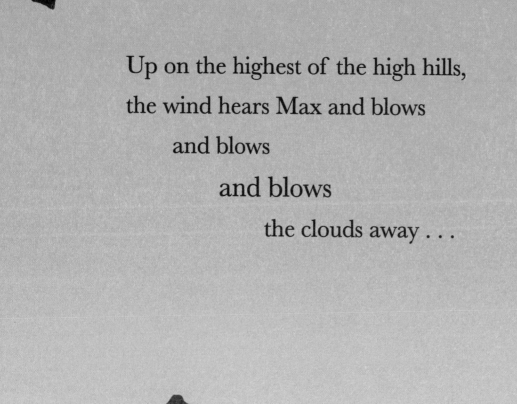

Up on the highest of the high hills,
the wind hears Max and blows
and blows
and blows
the clouds away . . .

And there, full and brilliant
in the night sky . . .

'Moon!'

'Goodnight Max,' whispers Moon.
'And thank you very much for coming.'

'Goodnight Moon,' yawns Max.
'It's been a long, long night,
now I can go to bed.'

'Max,' calls Moon across the night sky.
'Did you know that I **can** hear you
when you say goodnight at home?'

'Oh,' says Max. 'Now you tell me!
Well, **thank you**,
that's very good to know.'

Max is tired and happy.

He walks back along the rooftops . . .

and clambers down
the tall, tall tree.

Max creeps carefully over the sleeping dog,

and sleepy, very sleepy –
he climbs the stairs to bed.

'Sleep tight Max,' says Moon.

But Max doesn't hear.
Max is snoring,
    snoring,
        snoring, fast asleep.

for
Anouk

PUFFIN BOOKS
Published by the Penguin Group: London, New York,
Australia, Canada, India, Ireland, New Zealand and South Africa
Penguin Books Ltd, Registered Offices: 80 Strand, London WC2R 0RL, England
puffinbooks.com
First published 2015
001
Text and illustrations copyright © Ed Vere, 2015
Made and printed in China
Hardback ISBN: 978–0–723–29457–3
Paperback ISBN: 978–0–723–29915–8

edvere.com
@ed_vere